TO MY DEAREST DARLING.....

R. VISHNU

I dedicate this book to the one person who I call 'My dearest darling.....'

Contents

Foreword

Being the author's best friend I have seen him work on this book for hours together. This is not just a work of imagination rather this can be termed as a 'perfect bridge' between imagination and hands-on experience. The author has penned down what he had witnessed and had been a part of and used that as a core to develop the other parts of the story. The entire story revolves around this idea and the subsequent development is where the imagination of the author took over. In short- It is not just a story, it is also an autobiography.

Preface

Writing this book has not been easy. Being a 10th grader I had to seamlessly manage both studies as well as authoring the book. The story for this book is not something that pops up in your mind when taking a bath or cycling. This story was engineered specifically for readers who do not have time to read the entire book as well as this packs the emotional elements too. "To My Dearest Darling...." has in a way helped me to realise the true importance of the 'real darling' who was the reason this book was penned down.

Acknowledgements

It has never been a one-man job writing this book. I would like to thank Vimal Sibi for being the first person to have shared his thoughts on this story. Next would be Deepak Devanand for his unthankable contribution to editing the story. without him, the editing of this book would have been impossible. I would like to convey my deepest thanks to Murali Krishnan for always being the pillar of support that I had needed always.

Prologue

CHAPTER I

Chapter-1

He felt the pain, a drastic pain in his chest. For him, this was a blow that he could never manage. He looked as if he had seen all his dead ancestors come back to life to have tea with him. She was his only one and he had spent a great many days with her. This was the last thing he had expected in his life. His past flashed in front of his eyes where he stood in the middle of his school corridor unable to show any emotions.

It was a fine autumn day in the lovely countryside of Yorkshire. In the stately home "Hepworth House" lived Sinderby Hepworth, a countryman to whom the concept of marriage was unknown. He boasted of a business empire exceeding the combined wealth of many nations put together. At 40 years, one could conclude that he bore the worries of the entire world on his shoulders. His face had a few wrinkles, signs of his excessive work and he was a stone heavier than what was good for him. He was old fashioned for he used a half hunter pocket watch, loved the grouse season and still wrote letters sealed with his family crest. He loved things to be done the perfect way.

It was a usual Monday morning and Sinderby, being an early riser, woke up at 5 in the morning. There was not a single day in his entire life where he skipped his morning jog around the estate. He came back and took a leisurely bath. He loved his English Breakfast and would trade it for nothing, washed it all down with a cup of tea and started his journey to London, to hold the reins and steer Sinderby Corporation into another day of success. This was a man whose dreams came true already. He owned everything in life except one.

Sailing from across the pond in Cunard's Queen Mary 2 was a 21st-century modern girl. She was tall and slender and her hair was a bold chestnut. She had a face that worked like a magnet, only towards men. She too was 40 but looked a decade younger. Named after the sister ship in which she sailed, Elizabeth was sailing to Southampton to meet a person she dearly loved... maybe loves. During the 6th night of the 7day transatlantic voyage, Elizabeth dined with Ms Jarvis, a lady who refused to reveal her first name.

"It is so good of you to come to dine with us. Elizabeth" remarked Ms Jarvis with a hint of sarcasm.

"I am glad that you say that Ms Jarvis. I felt like dining in my room and being in solidarity all these days." Elizabeth stayed at the Queens Grill Suite and she loved to hang her collection of Picasso's and Monet's on the walls of her suite just so it gives her a homely feel.

"Do you travel transatlantic often?" enquired Ms Jarvis
"I travel if the need arises" came back the immediate reply from Elizabeth.

Two more people joined their table, a Mr Bottlehead and Mr Karl. Mr . Bottlehead was a Yankee and always spoke about the United States and why it is best while Mr Karl being a German answered some questions and spoke only when he was spoken to. That dinner went smooth with no bumps and finally, everyone retired to their beds.

The next morning Queen Mary 2 docked in Southampton and Elizabeth was among the first of the few passengers to disembark. She did not want to see the companions of her dinner again in the morning. Immediately after she got down, she hired a cab and went straight to Southampton Central, hopped on the

SouthWestern and reached London Waterloo. She got down and checked in on Claridge's Prince Alexander Suite. She did not have the time to rest and relax in the beauty of the Suite, she was here with a plan and she had to execute it.

Sinderby's office room can be compared to a Victorian-era sitting room. He had a Queen Anne desk adorned with sealing wax, ink dip pen, letters and envelopes- everything would look out of proportion just outside his room. He gave the impression that he was a Conservative while his brain was an enigma and a supercomputer put together. He was not averse to change but ready to accept it if it meant business would boom. Just as he sat behind his desk, his secretary William arrived in his room.

"What is in my diary today William?"

"First the annual board meeting Sir. You had asked me to brief you about item 4, after that the usual rounds and you have a lunch appointment with Mr Richard Sharp, Chairman of the BBC. After lunch, you have 30 minutes free time following which you have to make the financial year speech to the stockholders and that's all for today, sir."

"Well.... That is quite easy and I want no one to disturb me during the meeting. Is that clear?"

" Yes sir and can I gather the board, sir?"

"Yes."

Elizabeth came out of the building and hired another cab, she was looking fine but still doubted her plan. She had an adrenaline rush. She was going to meet this person after 25 years and the last time she saw him, he was in his teens and was a schoolboy. She resisted the urge to cancel her plan, she even gave it a thought but dismissed it immediately and gave the driver an address and asked him to take her there as quickly as possible.

Thc board meeting had started and the first item was 'Security'. Sir Edward was the Head of Security and he was not in a very good mood. The Vice-Chairman opened the board meeting by firing his first question, "Sir Edward, the security of our top tier members, which unfortunately includes you, I and the Chairman himself have been infiltrated not once but twice in the past month, I hope you have a perfectly reasonable explanation for all this." Sir Edward rose and said with an obvious weakness in his voice, "The infiltrations were quite strong and have given us key information on the loopholes which can be exploited in our system, we will look into it....." "He looks as if he needs a whisky." suggested the Financial Secretary. Suddenly all the emergency alarms started blaring in high pitched noise. Red coloured sirens started blinking all over the boardroom. All the board members were in a state of panic, one of them took out his Beretta which was strapped to his legs while another lady took a Glock. All their tensions settled down when William entered the room and shut the alarms off. They left a sigh of relief and were relaxed.

"What is all this nonsense, Will?"

"It is not Mr Sinderby" William turned around to face all the board members and said, "My sincerest apologies to the members, it was I who turned on the alarms and I have a perfectly simple reason to do so." He again turned back to face Sinderby, "Sir, you better meet this person. I assure you it will not be in vain"

"Will, you disrupt my meeting so I get to see a nit-wit? Ask whoever it may be to get an appointment first"

"It is she and I bet my fortune, sir, you need to see her."

"I am agreeing to see her just so I can get the pleasure of seeing your fortune reduced substantially" barked Sinderby and he rose to go back to his office.

CHAPTER II

Chapter-2

When he saw who it was on his CCTV, he could not believe his eyes and buzzed for William.

"Shall I show her in sir?"

"You bloody well show her in"

"Yes sir"

The doorman announced "Elizabeth Sinclair"

Just as Elizabeth walked inside the room and towards Sinderby, he stood up and his heart skipped a beat. Sweat trickled down from his forehead despite the a/c being on. He could not believe his eyes and left his jaw wide open. He felt nervous, happy and sad, all at the same time. She brought with her everything that would make Sinderby a complete man. It was a great success for William for his fortune was to be doubled. She stood in front of Sinderby with her head high and eyes straight but no one could know that she was equally as nervous as Sinderby was. There was a moment's silence and Elizabeth broke it.

"How are you, Sinderby?"

Sinderby could not muster up the courage nor could he find the words to answer that question. He gulped down a triple scotch and fell back on his chair like an apple falling from a tree. She became scared and William ran to rescue the Chairman.

"I am fine Will, Sinderby will always stand firmly on his legs."

William helped him to sit back in his chair.

"Will, could you please close the door on your way back?"

William understood the sign and left them all alone. It

was an intense moment between both the parties Elizabeth was still standing and Sinderby took another triple scotch. Finally, it was his turn to break the silence.

"Dearest Darling.... Will, you bally well kiss me?" His voice sounded like he had not been in touch with humanity and was seeing the first human in a decade.

"Sure why not" came back the immediate reply.

They both were seeing each other after 25 years and he just could not come to accept the fact that he had finally seen his sister and she was happy, happy as a lark.

Sinderby stood up and guided her to an adjoining sitting room and offered her a comfortable armchair as he sat opposite it. By now he was fine and was in a position to speak clearly and was out of the shock of seeing his sister and was happy to see her.

"Would you like to have a cup of something?"

"I would prefer some coffee"

He rang for his pantry and ordered coffee. He could not hide his surprise at seeing her and felt that his chest would explode with all that happiness. She on the other hand remained calm and serene, characteristics an elder sister is bound to possess.

"What made you come to England and me?"

"Am I not allowed to visit my brother?"

"Of course not, You are always welcome to visit me and to see England"

"That cheers me up a bit"

The doorbell rang and a maid entered with a tray carrying a coffee pot and 2 polished silver cups.

"I like the way you treat me, Sinderby, like an outsider."

"Like what?"

"You try to impress me by giving me coffee in silver pots and a tray made with ivory from African elephants, this won't do darling."

Sinderby sulked for a minute thinking that he had disappointed her.

"I am not impressing you sister, I give coffee to everyone in this same way!"

"You know what I would like? Take me out for dinner, but not in any of those fancy Ritz or Claridges. Take me out for dinner in the streets of London."

"I am not sure I can manage that, I need to take my security detail with me wherever I go and my entourage cannot enter the crowded streets."

"Can you not do at least this to your sister? What are you good for then? I came here to enjoy with you but you have so many excuses up your sleeves, I think I will just go back to the US."

"No, don't ever do that! I will take you to Camden market today evening, be ready by 7 PM."

"Now that is like the boy I know, ok then I leave you to it."

"Wait wait, where are you staying and where should I pick you up?"

"I'll come here, you no need to worry about that, how is that you guys say it? Ah yes, chap"

She left his office and went back to her hotel with a sense of satisfaction and pride while Sinderby was left in a cloud of daze and amazement.

Sinderby finished his work early and went to his London home. He was sure that using a car would not be feasible hence he decided to rent a moped. He threw away his suit and tie, removed his half hunter, and wore a beige coloured medium spread shirt and jeans. To his valet, this was a person who he had never seen before and his security stopped him to verify his identity. Sinderby had evolved and became a new man, his sister has had a great deal of impact on him. He took the moped and went to his office. He hid behind a bush so that no one would be able to identify him. He was afraid that if any of his employees found him in this fashion, he would risk losing the respect that he had built all these years and that his firm might lose all the standards for which they are known. He peaked and looked around to find his sister, his hands rustling against the hedges but he did not seem to mind, all that he wanted now was to find her. Seemingly out of nowhere came a hand and tapped on his shoulders and he turned around scared, he caught his heart when the hand tapped him only to find out that Elizabeth was there.

"What are you doing here?"

"Waiting for you."

"So shall we start?"

"Yes sure"

The sister-brother duo travelled to Camden market to enjoy dinner. To Sinderby, this was a great step down from all the white tie and tails dinner that he was used to, yet he accepted it because he wanted his sister to be happy. His happiness lies in her happiness. It was he who drove the moped and to his surprise, he drove it well and many did not recognize him.

"What do you think of this place darling, the cheese wheel?" asked Elizabeth

"Sounds good, why not give it a try?"

"Na na na, I decide that dear bro, I decide that."

"Fine then but I am famished."

"I see, fine we will dine here." She could not bring herself to see her dear brother suffering from hunger and wanted to put him out of his misery immediately.

They went in and Sinderby's stomach was a trifle empty and all he needed now was some food. They immediately

ordered.
"I will take a red sauce pasta with some cabernet sauvignon," she said.
"White sauce with Chardonnay" was his choice.

"I hope that this place makes you feel better sis."
"It is not the place that I am fond of dear, I had an instinct that you felt too high for your boots, I wanted to bring you down, I am sorry if I had made a mistake."
He placed a finger on her lips and said, "Look here Liz, Who am I? Your brother right? As my sister you bloody have all the rights to correct me and never apologise to me, is that clear?"
She nodded in agreement.
"It is nice to see the real you after so many days, how did you live without me for all these years?" Sinedery preferred not to answer that question and luckily their dinner arrived and he got a chance to change the topic.
"How did you come to England? You must have flown, I presume."
"Then you presume wrong, I sailed."
"Sailed?"
"Yes, aboard the Queen Mary 2"
"I see and you had a nice journey?"
"Oh yes, yes."
"That's nice darling sister."
Between mouthfuls of pasta and wine, they chatted about everything from London to New York, Real estate, ships and whatnot.

"Finished your pasta?"
"Yes Liz"
"Want to dance?"
"Well... er it is quite an invigorating proposal but... well"
"Yes or no?" Her voice was full of enthusiasm and he did

not want to spoil that.

"Yes!"

They drove to the Hawley's arms and danced and drank till their knees become weak and their minds turned pale. That night he was not in a proper state to drive and she was not even in a state that could be quite described as proper. He called William and asked him to take care of the moped. To William's surprise, this was the first time he had seen his employer and friend drink this much. He took the moped and called for Sinderby's Rolls to drop both of them in his London residence.

When Sinderby woke up, it was already 9 in the morning and she was still asleep. He was in such a state that he just draped himself in whatever piece of clothing was available to him, he did not even care to think if it was decent or not and ran down the steps as if he was running to catch the last train to heaven. Just as he came down William entered and said,

"Today has been declared a holiday for the corporation sir. You could not manage it, but do not worry as the stock monitoring team is working on shifts so they will not plummet like your manners yesterday night."

Sinderby gave out a sigh of relief,

"Firstly, Thank you for handling the situation yesterday, if it were not for you I would have been behind bars right now!"

William sarcastically said, "Yes I see the headlines on the Guardian, 'Sinderby Hepworth jailed'.

"Oh shut up Will, for god's sake, and secondly, Thank you again for taking care of today. Finally, I did not let my manners plummet, my sister wanted to have an all-night out and I could not help it."

"You love your sister so much, sir?"

"Yes and do come in, sit and have a cuppa, I make good tea,

and I will say how dearly I love her."

William obliged and came in. Sinderby went up and came down again but this time properly dressed and went to the kitchen and made a hot steaming cuppa and gave it to William. He took the sofa just opposite him.

"Sir, might I suggest something?"

"Go on"

"The corporation is doing extremely well and the board members are on their annual holiday, so why not utilise this time to give your sister something memorable?"

"Sounds good but where shall I take her? She has seen everything England has to offer."

"Has she been to Scotland?"

"Scotland?"

"Yes"

"Marvellous suggestion Will, simply extraordinary! I will take her to Scotland and we'll stay there for a week."

"So when do you plan to start sir?"

"Why not today afternoon?"

"Sure sir, I will make all the arrangements."

Sinderby was in a state of joy and he threw his arms up in the air to celebrate it. He then went up to wake her up to break the news to her.

"Dearest Darling, please wake up. It is 9 in the morning."

"Why so soon?" Came back with the reply. She sounded as if she had hit the bed just an hour ago.

"It is late already sis, do wake up," he said gently. She acknowledged but did not react. He felt like a proud father waking up his daughter. He prayed to God that if he ever had the boon of having another birth, his sister had to be reincarnated as his daughter.

After 15 minutes she woke up and came down.

"Where is my coffee?" she asked with a yawn that made the tone of the big ben a melody to the ears.

"No coffee, only tea."

"Fine."

"Want to go out?"

"No, I am dead from inside out after yesterday."

"Nah, I did not mean that kind of going out."

"What did you mean then?"

"Well... I have asked William to arrange for a journey to Scotland...I hope you would like it."

She gave an expression that consisted of a smile, a smirk and a hint of joy combined with anger. One could not decrypt the message that she wanted to convey, well that is one reason why we say the female brain is uncomparable.

Sinderby's expression changed suddenly, he felt he had made a mistake by arranging the tour.

"Have I made a mistake sis? Are you not comfortable with this plan? Say no more, I am cancelling it."

Just as he was about to reach out to the cell phone, she jumped in like a monkey and caught his hands.

"No, don't cancel it!"

"But you said you are not comfortable with it?" The wonder in his eyes and face was so cute that she found it adorable.

"I did not say so. It is just that you could have said this earlier to me, but it is decided so it has to be done! When are we leaving?"

"Today afternoon"

"That does not leave us with much time. Have you packed your bags?"

"There is no need for that, I have a Scottish wardrobe purchased and it is in the residence."

"What do you expect me to wear? Your tails?"

"Um...No, but I have purchased a female Scottish wardrobe too, exclusively for you."

This was her turn to be bewildered.

"I am not sure I got you, YOU purchased a wardrobe for ME? When?"

"Today morning. I knew we would not be having time to pack so I placed an order for a set of female formal and informal clothes and it would have arrived before we even reached there."

She was impressed by this gesture of his and she came around the couch and stood opposite him looking directly in the eye. He looked back but he was like a fish out of water and his look was like a baby looking toward the mother. She hugged him and kissed him on the cheek and he felt that moment to be the best of his entire life. He did not feel this happy when he was declared the richest man in the UK, he did not feel this happy when his name was announced on the New Year's honours list. He felt this happy only when his sister kissed him. This was something really valuable to him and he would die to experience this kiss just another time.

They dressed up and drove to Heathrow where they boarded the Gulfstream G800, Sinderby's private short-haul jet. He had personally customised the interior in such a way that the aircraft's interior reflected upon the heritages, culture and history of the British isle.

"This is nice bro."

"Oh thank you."

"I never knew you had a private jet."

"Well I rarely use them and if I ever need to fly, I fly on my own so there is never the need to travel luxuriously when it is just me."

"You know how to fly?"

"Yes, I can steer a commercial plane with ease."

"Well, I am astounded by your ability. Will you ever fly me?"

"Oh sure, why not."

Just as they settled the jet's exclusive air hostess, Linda came in. She was a slender figure and her hair was a bold black that cascaded down and reached her shoulders like a beautiful waterfall. She had all the characteristics of a perfect air hostess.

"What would you like to drink, sir? Madam?"

While Sinderby preferred Krug 1988, a rare vintage, she on the other hand, out of all the beverages the plane had to offer, settled for a cuppa.

The plane taxied and was on the runway ready to take off. The pilot turned on the intercom system and made the following announcement,

"Good day passengers, I am Clive, your captain along with James, the copilot. Today we will be flying to Scotland, landing at Glasgow International. The flight time will be approximately an hour and a half. We may be facing some rough winds on our journey and we will try our best to bypass them please pay attention to the seatbelt sign. Thank you."

The duo felt the plane accelerate like a cheetah in search of her prey and their stomach felt an unusually uncomfortable juggle and there it was, suddenly out of nowhere the plane took off into the skies above London. Both Sinderby and Elizabeth admired the view of London from the skies and they settled down comfortably in their seats by the time the plane reached its cruising altitude. Sinderby felt relaxed at 40,000 feet up in the air as he was casually sipping through his glass of champagne, to him it was heaven. He never wanted anything to be loud and attention seeking. He relaxed the most during this journey, but for Elizabeth sitting simply was not fun, it was sheer torture. It had just been 15 minutes after taking off and she already felt as if she had been bored to death. Slowly yet steadily she broke the silence.

"Do you think we can play a game?"

"Why? Yes, sure. I have the plane stocked with cards, we could always make a great game out of blackjacks!"

"Why are you so stupid all the time?"

"Have I offended you, my dearest treasure?"

"You are still self-absorbed and you want to play blackjack! For god's sake, grow up!"

"I am sorry. Why don't you suggest what game to play"

To him, this was a relatively safe move.

"Why don't we play some good old chess? Or even monopoly?"

"I am fine with monopoly."

"Thought you'd say that, but fine with me."

Sinderby was relieved that he had not offended her once again. After 45 minutes Linda once again reappeared taking the passengers' order for their lunch.

"What would you prefer to have, ma'am?"

From the already curated menu, she picked the Gravadlax With Celeriac & Fennel Salad for starters and selected Grilled garlic and black pepper shrimp for the main course and washed all that down with a cup of chocolate ice cream- she had taken too many drinks for a plane journey. Sinderby was very picky in regards to his food, he hired the best cook and always travelled to any destination where he had no control over the food with his cook. For his starters, it was Carpaccio Scallops, and his main course was Grilled scallops with cream corn and finished with a classic lemon tart.

After lunch with just 30 minutes left on the journey, they got ready to touch down on Scottish soil. The journey was relatively smooth with no terrible turbulence. It was smooth and relaxing. The G800 seamlessly touched down on the runway of Glasgow airport and Elizabeth personally thanked the pilots and air hostess-something Sinderby would never do. He saw all this from the safety of the tinted windows in his Rolls which he had boarded just as soon as the plane touched down and the doors were opened. He reflected on how poorly he had treated his staff who took great care of him. For the first time in his life, he felt guilt.

CHAPTER III

Chapter-3

She joined him on the back of the Rolls and they started their journey into the highlands. Sinderby had hired the Donglen House, situated in the Cairngorms National Park and which was once owned by Sir Billy Connoly.

The car took a serene turn into the entrance and the pathway leading towards the doorsteps of the grand house. All the 12 staff were waiting out in a unique semicircle formation with the highest ranks towards the left which can be seen from the clothing to the lowest on the right to welcome the master and mistress of this grand mansion for the duration of the next 7 days.

The butler took the lead and introduced himself,

"Good day sir, good day madam, I am Peter, the butler of Donglen House, and this is Jhon, the under butler."

"Under Butler!" Sinderby and Elizabeth cried in unison. They were shocked to acknowledge the fact that there remained under butlers.

Knowing their shock, Peter quickly said, "We like things to be run properly in Donglen Sir, and we are ready to make sure it is picture-perfect."

"Bravo Peter, bravo!" was Sinderby's reaction while Elizabeth remained without any reaction.

"Shall we go in sir?"

"Sure why not?"

The party went inside and Peter helped them to remove their coats. Donglen was indeed the unsung beauty of the highlands. Once someone enters the house, they can never even think about leaving it. Peter jumped in,

"Sir your valet, Bernard, will be waiting for you in the Anderson Bedroom sir and for you madam, a Lady's maid, Ms Jannet is appointed in your bedroom."

Sinderby was impressed by the standards that were maintained in Donglen while Elizabeth did not show any reactions. Spending most of her time in the United States, she did not care to uphold the culture and tradition of these great houses; rather in them she saw loads of money being wasted, she did not understand that the job of such houses was to be a source of employment for the surrounding yet she did not want to comment on it and for once held her tongue. She did not want all this hard work of her little brother to go in vain nor to dishearten him.

Peter showed them the rooms, starting with the drawing room and going all the way to the games room and the whisky room and finished the tour with the dining room and the library. They both liked the house and went into their respective bedrooms to change. Sinderby quickly got acquainted with his valet and he helped him to get into a comfortable shirt and trousers and relieved him from his travel wear. On the other hand, Elizabeth used Jannet just to style her hair and she did the dressing all by herself.

It was almost 7 in the evening, to keep up appearances Sinderby had invited his dearest friend in the highlands, Mr and Ms Alastair. Mr Alastair and Sinderby were close friends in their school. The Alastair's came in a stylish Aston and Peter opened the doors of the car to welcome the guests. Sinderby was standing at the doorsteps and welcomed him with wide arms.

"How are you dear old chap Alastair? How the bloody hell are you?"

"I am fine, Sinderby, in the pink of health! How are you?"

"Oh, I am something. My business keeps me alive and it is my sister who gives me the real thrill of the chase. I hope you know what I mean?"

"Surely, How can I ever forget it?"

"Ms Alastair, how are you?"

"I am great Mr. Sinderby."

"Oh please do call me Sinderby, no need for Mr."

"Sure."

"Please come in, Please."

He showed them into the library where they had gathered.

"Oh and before I forget, this is more or less like a surprise for her, she does not know that I have invited you guys down here for dinner."

"That is very thoughtful of you, Sinderby," remarked Alastair. They all sat down in a comfortable armchair by the fire in the library and Peter served them sherry.

Elizabeth came down to the library and she was in for a surprise. When her eyes met the first glimpse of Alastair, she did not know what to do. Her heart started to beat quicker than usual and her pulse rate dwindled with her sense of manners decreasing second by second. She looked as if she needed a whisky and she did not hesitate to drink it for her life depended on it. After all that Alastair had done to her and her brother, she was bound to have a drink if it meant that it would save her. She relieved herself quickly, came to her senses and greeted them with joy on her face although one does not surely know what was the feeling in her heart.

"Alastair! How are you?

"I am great Elizabeth. I think you have not met my wife, Greta."

"Greta, so nice to meet you. How do you do?"

"I am great, thank you."
Elizabeth found it a tad bit uncomfortable to relax and enjoy in the presence of Alastair. She caught her brother when he went to get another glass of sherry and whispered in his ears, "Did you need to invite that fellow here? Was it necessary? After all that he had....." Sinderby stopped her abruptly and said, "I know what you mean Liz, he said he has a plan and that he would like to propose it to is sort of an apology. Let's give him a chance and see, after all, we are not kids anymore." Elizabeth was not quite sure but she was confident that they were capable of handling the situation.

Peter came in and announced dinner. The party of 4 gathered in the extravagant dining room. It was adorned with grand chandeliers and the walls were completed with traditional Scottish chequered templates and the same applied to the chairs. The dining table was made out of mahogany- something that Sinderby seemed to like. They all took their seats with Sinderby on the head, to his right he had Greta and to his left was Elizabeth, just beside Greta, Alastair was placed. The menu for dinner included Cullen Skink, Lobster, Grouse and traditional Haggis-Simple yet elegant.

It was during dinner that Alastair wanted to announce his apology. He said, "My dear friend Sinderby and his dear sister Elizabeth, I know that I am a wronged man in this house and that you will never forgive me for my sins.." He said this facing Elizabeth and her face spoke pages, She was satisfied that he understood his mistake but she was sad and tensed as being the object of the target. "... I do hope that it is time for me to make my apology, so I have spoken with Lord Howard, a dear friend of mine, to invite you for the Christmas Party in Castle Howard."

To Sinderby this was great news and indeed yes, he rejoiced in it. “My dear chap, thank you so very much for this. Thank you.” Elizabeth did not understand what Castle Howard was or what a Christmas party meant, all that she could understand was Alastair had done a good deed as reparations for his past blunders and she was happy that he was changing. After dinner, all of them went into the Whisky room for some wine and it was already terribly late, hence the Alastair’s bid their goodbyes and left Donglen. It was now just the two very loving brother and sister.

Sinderby came in thinking back on how the dinner went. He was happy to catch up with the one and only friend he had when he was in school. To him, this was a great experience. He went into the whisky room and she was sitting there motionless. “What is it Liz?” he asked. “Do we need to go to Castle Howard brother?” He sensed a tone of sadness in her voice. He did not want to sadden his only sister nor did he want to decline the offer of his only friend. He sunk into a closeby armchair and started to think about what to do. In 15 minutes he said these words, “Dearest darling, we will go this once and if you find uncomfortable anytime during the middle of the party or in the future, just say the words ‘Fedora hat’ and we will leave the party, irrespective of any guest in the room and any level of formality the party demands.” She thought for a second that he had rehearsed every word of this small speech sometime in the past 15 minutes and the result was this. She however did like the terms of this deal. “I agree to it,” she said. “Then consider that we have a deal!”

Having secured her involvement in the Christmas party, she bid him goodnight and went to her bedroom. He sat in the whisky room with no one to disturb him, thinking about everything that he had seen and faced in his life, just about everything.

In the morning, she woke up and went down to have tea. She had wanted to see the gardens early in the morning after tea. She was surprised to find Sinderby still in the Whisky room awake. "Whatever is the matter with you, Sinderby?" she asked with a sisterly concern in her voice. "I did not feel like sleeping, Liz."

"Is there any problem? Are you all right?"

"I am fine darling, I am fine. I am just sane but I am fine." Elizabeth burst out laughing. When he asked her why she was laughing, she said, "I always thought that you were a sane little brother, I am finally glad to know that you have acknowledged it."

He laughed and said that he had read a book and did not want to sleep.

"Whatever on earth has made you wake up so early in the morning?" he inquired. "I wanted to see the gardens, they were so beautiful yesterday." He was at first taken aback to know that SHE had taken INTEREST in gardens, later recovered knowing that she could change her interests just as how she changed outfits. He asked her, "Do you mind coming out with me today? I have some properties that I want to show you?" "Sure" came back the reply.

"When can we start?"

"Around 10?"

"Sure bro."

He changed and came down, waited for his sister, once she came down he started his journey into Scotland. He gave the driver the day off and drove the car on his own. This somehow seemed to surprise Elizabeth. "Why are you driving on your own?"

"I did not want a third person to know where I was going."

"Sounds fair."

After an hour the car took a steep turn into 'Sinderby Mansion'. The large Georgian structure stood on its grounds and it demanded a great respect-just from its owner. From the outside, it looked just as marvellous as it was from the inside. One can never stop appreciating the beauty of this mansion. Elizabeth found this more likeable than Donglen castle. When he brought the car to a halt she immediately got down and started admiring the beauty and the opulence of the mansion.

"Why did you not take me here for this vacation? Why Donglen?"

"I just felt like going there rather than here."

"I simply love this place! Oh, nothing can stop me from falling for this beauty!"

Sinderby felt happy on seeing his sister enjoying herself. Elizabeth showed herself inside and did not care to wait for her brother. He walked behind her slowly. She liked everything about the mansion. The gardens were lovely and the rooms were exquisite, there was nothing that she disliked. As she settled down after her short excursion she asked him the one question that was taunting her all this while.

"Why have you brought me here?"

"Shall we discuss the answer over a cup of tea?"

"Sure, why not?"

He rang for some tea and while they were waiting Elizabeth stole herself and ventured to the library where she found books about the history of the Hepworths. Just as she took a book to read he called out to her. Disappointed, yet excited to know the answer to her question, she went there.

"So now, what is the answer?"
He thought about the words that he was going to say and finally said, "You know these great structures and mansions and my business empire, literally everything that I own or have inherited must be passed on." Smiling, thinking that she had got the gist of his message she asked, "I understand, who is that lucky girl?" For a minute he was baffled, bewildered and confused, when he understood what she had meant, he was quick to jump in, "No Liz, no, it is not that. Please do not interrupt me, let me finish, please." After a brief pause, he continued, " As I was saying, all these things must be passed on to someone else, but I do not wish to enter into matrimony nor adopt a child. I have thought for days on end and I have finalised two candidates who will inherit all that, that is now mine and I am glad to inform you that, it is you who will be the heiress to all this, the second candidate being your other brother, Carlton."

Her eyes widened and although she was in such a rage that she would have slapped him in the face, she held her temper. She knew how important this was. "I hope that I have taken the right decision in making you in charge of all this when....when I am not with you and I sincerely hope that you would accept it."

She had a sense of guilt, she felt she was not the right person to inherit all this and that he needed a family. She was confident that she could make him come around. "I think that you need a family and you must be happy with them. As you said all this must be passed on, decide wisely on who must inherit it." Without thinking for a second and with the satisfaction that he had already expected this question, Sinderby fired his best shot, "But you are my family darling, you are all that I have!" He hoped this would be enough to make her decide-a a grave mistake. Elizabeth, still sure that she should not be the heiress, said in a massive stroke, "I understand Mr Hepworth..." The selection of words made him already nervous and he was not sure what to do. His heart was pounding like a beast. "....But we are not even blood-related!" He lost it. He was sad and he was sure that any more protest would go in vain. He sulked down on his sofa, thinking deeply for some time. She too sat down. He rose, gave out a breath, a crisp one, and said, "Dear Ms Elizabeth, I am sorry for troubling you in matters that do not concern you. It was stupid of me to have brought you into the picture. I sincerely hope that you will stay till Christmas to honour our dinner appointment at Castle Howard, after that you are free to go. Good Morning." He stormed out of the mansion and went to the gardens. He could not bring himself to face her in the eye-something that he had faced 2 decades ago. He had to hold his tears when he gave out this speech. Sitting on the swing in the garden, he was crying out. He had never once wished to cause her pain, and now when she had betrayed him, what was left? He would have gladly gulped down a whisky.

She thought to herself that she should have not brought that topic here. He was having his time and she felt she had ruined it for him. All that he wanted to do was to give her everything and she could have refused it decently without bringing sadness to anyone yet she thought her actions were disgraceful. She wanted to ask for forgiveness. She ran out to the terrace to have a bird's view of the mansion to find out where he was. All that she knew was he went out but there was a question to which she did not have an answer. She saw him sulk down in the garden swing and ran to see him. When she reached there however she was greeted by an envelope addressed to her. She did not want to think about anything. With trembling hands like that of a drunkard, she picked up the envelope and found that it was not sealed or glued, meaning he knew she would read it as soon as possible. When her fingers reached the inside of the envelope she felt the papers, with haste she removed them and opened them. It went as,

Dear Elizabeth,

I saw with my very own eyes how dearly you loved this mansion as opposed to Donglen. I might have been a disappointment to you but I do not want your stay to be a disappointment as well. I have ordered for your luggage to be transported here and they will reach you by evening. I have also attached with this the cards of the best clothes shops around- I know you have the money, but I was and am sure that you do not know where to get clothes. I will no longer be staying at Donglen, so please do not come in search of me. I will be sending a car a day before Christmas to attend the grand dinner. If you are still staying in the mansion, do get into it, if you have started for the States, please make sure the driver knows it.

Yours sincerely,

Sinderby.

She looked around to find that the car had gone away. Her eyes were filled with tears and she wanted to run and chase the car and she did that. Seeing her run towards the gate like a madwoman, the butler came out running to her. Just as she was about to get out of the mansion grounds, he caught her and asked her to stay. "Madam, what are you doing?"

"Leave me alone! I said leave me bloody alone!" came back the reply. She was as mad as a hornet. "Madam, please come back, I beg you!" "I will not come back until I have managed to stop his car!" "Madam, Sinderby sir will be back here very soon ma'am!" After some considerable persuasion, shc finally dropped the idea of a chase and settled on the indoor balcony on the second floor. Whenever she saw a car going by she would assume that it would be him coming back but it was always to her disappointment. Days went by and weeks rolled in, and slowly she changed. She went down to the dining hall to dine rather than eat at the pub by the road. After a fortnight, she changed completely and went along with the staff and the neighbours of the mansion. She was viewed as a friendly figure. Occasionally she would break down and cry about her fault but the others would soothe her saying that it was a genuine mistake and it will be solved.

Sinderby paid the cheque and settled the bill for their 2 days and one night stay and packed his bags. He was constantly reminded of their 'breakup' and wanted to cry but he held his tears. He was a man known to control and suppress his emotions. He had a serene smile on his face and ordered his car to take him to Glasgow airport. When he boarded his plane to London, Linda asked him, "Sir, where is madam?" He looked at her and replied, "She has gone for her constitution." During the entire hour and a half journey to London, he did not eat nor drink anything, he just stared out of the window looking at the sky. When the plane touched down, he boarded out, got into the back seat of his Bently and simply drove away-he forgot to remove his luggage from the plane. He was so preoccupied with the thought of her on his journey back. When he reached London, William asked, "Why are you back so early sir?" He replied, "It went poorly Will......we fell out." The next day when he came to his office he was not able to focus on anything, anything as simple as a lunch appointment. He always felt distracted and disturbed. During dinner, he somehow managed to pour an entire bottle of whisky on his dinner jacket and ate his dinner without being aware of what he had done. The next morning when he woke up he realised that he must do something about it or else he would lose his sanity. He decided that he would focus all his sadness and sorrow on his work, in the sense all the energy consumed by these sorrows will be diverted towards productivity. That day went particularly well, although he could not improve his social skills. Days went by. Finally, when he woke up and looked at the calendar it was the 24th of December.

CHAPTER IV

Chapter-4

On Christmas eve she was waiting for the car to appear. She had prepared the speech that she would say to him when she would meet him and rehearsed it line by line. She was usually not a heavy drinker but on that day she finished the entire rack of claret and half a rack of sherries. Her nervousness knew no bounds and she grew restless hour by hour.

He finished his work by 3 PM and went to Heathrow. This time instead of flying private he flew commercial. He reached Scotland and went up to his mansion. No one could identify him despite their best efforts. He heard people murmur, "The face looks familiar..." With a moustache, a long beard and half-moon spectacles he could throw everyone off the scent.

At half-past 5, when Elizabeth gave up any hope of seeing Sinderby's car, he came in an Aston and honked in front of the Mansion gates. One could never express her happiness on seeing the car. She ran down the stairs and found that the entire household had gathered to send her off. The butler and the cook were a personal favourite of Elizabeth. Both of them said that Herself and Sinderby were good souls and such small breakups were bound to come between friends. She bid her final goodbyes to them and got into the car. She could not recognize that it was indeed Sinderby driving the car and this could be attributed to his first-class makeup and his ability to switch between accents. Elizabeth was surprised when she noticed the car did not take the turn towards Glasgow airport. She asked,

"Are we not flying?"
He replied in a bold Scottish accent, "No ma'am. Sir has given me strict orders that I am to drive you to London." He also produced a letter signed by him which was written just an hour ago and repeated what he just said. "Fine then."

To spark up a conversation, she asked him, "Do you have any children?" Baffled by this question but not wanting to blow his cover he went with the flow and said, "Oh yes ma'am. I have 3 daughters and 2 sons." For a split second, she was taken aback. "Really?" she asked. "Yes ma'am." came back the reply. "Why do you have so many children? Is it even logistically feasible for you?" "Well yes ma'am, however, I cannot answer the first part of your question," he said. A smile appeared on her face. They quickly became best friends and Sinderby quite forgot about the sadness that he had all these days and they were constantly chatting about everything they saw and came across. It was around 7 in the evening and she said, "I am hungry, do you know any good restaurants on the way?" He took this opportunity and said, "there are no restaurants here ma'am but if you are really hungry I can make you a cuppa, a toast with some baked beans and 2 boiled eggs." "That would be a treat!" she rejoiced. He pulled aside, opened the boot of the car and seemingly out of nowhere produced all the above-said food. "This is heaven for a hungry soul like me!" She cried. He stood there and watched as she devoured his dinner. After she gave out a loud and uncanny burp, she asked, "What about you? What will you have for dinner?"He said, "I never eat dinner ma'am. My wife thought I might get hungry and packed this for me." "May God bless your wife!" She said. It was his turn to smile now.

They smiled and he started again. 15 minutes into the journey he noticed that she had dozed off. He stopped the car, made her sleep comfortably, utilising the entire back seat and tucked her nicely with a comfortable duck feather rug. She slept like a child and he took a minute to shed a tear of joy and happiness. They reached London and he woke her up. “Madam, wake up” “Have we reached London?” “Yes, ma’am”. She woke up but was half asleep, walked into Sinderby’s London home and fell into the bed.

The following morning when she woke up she understood what had happened the previous night. She ran down to find Sinderby and he was indeed there. She was so desperate to meet him that she forgot the obvious that was staring her in the face. When she finally saw him face to face, and when he saw her face to face, both of them were sure that either one of them was about to cry. Like a bullet of a gun, both of them cried at the same time and it was he who first hugged her. “I am sorry sister. I am so sorry!” “No, it is I who must ask for an apology.” She demanded. “Whoever might have made a mistake darling, we will dwell on it later, for now, I wish you a Merry Christmas.” “Oh, how stupid of me, how stupid of me, I did not even care to think that it is Christmas today!” She paused for a minute. “Wishing you a Merry Christmas my dear brother and a very happy New Year!

After resolving all their conflicts and making peace with each other, they both had a hearty breakfast and enjoyed themselves indoors. They watched a movie and went out shopping. She asked him a question, “ Who was that driver you sent me yesterday? He was a nice chap.” After a moment he replied, “I have a small confession to make..... You see...er....the fact is I was your driver yesterday.” After a brief pause, he spoke in a Scottish accent, “Hello ma’am, how was your day?” Along with anger and surprise laughter too came out bustling from her. She beat him hard laughing,

"You bloody rascal!" She loved him dearly for driving her all the way. Then she realised that only him, such a sought after brother would tuck his sis and make sure that she slept comfortably. She shed a tear of love for him. That evening they dressed up, it was the biggest party ever for Elizabeth. For Sinderby White Tie parties were usual and he liked them. She dressed in a grand white ball gown which cascaded like a diamond waterfall to her back and reached the floor. She wore a diamond-encrusted necklace and off white gloves. She was informed well in advance that the evening would include strenuous dancing hence she selected an appropriate shoe. Sinderby was waiting below the stairs when he first caught a glimpse of her. Her beautiful eyes caught his attention. They were twinkling like the diamonds in her necklace. Her white ball gown was superbly made to order and fitted her perfectly. When she came down and stood opposite him, he was out of words to describe her and stood fixed on her beauty. "Will you say how I look or stand here like a statue?" "I would say how beautiful you are looking but then, sadly I am not able to find the words to express your beauty darling." That was surely a masterstroke. They climbed into the smart Bentley Azure and started the journey to Castle Howard.

Lord and Lady Howard were welcoming all the guests personally. They noticed the Bently and came down the steps. Sinderby swung the car around the entrance and came to a halt. One of the many footmen standing there opened the door to let Elizabeth out of the car. He gave the key to a valet standing nearby and turned his face to meet his host and hostess. "Good Evening Lord Howard, Lady Howard. How are you?"

"We are fine Mr Sinderby, how do you do?" "I am doing great m'lord. I think you have not met my sister, Ms

Elizabeth Sinclarie." "We have not had the pleasure of meeting her...." said Lord Hepworth and turned his glance towards her. She curtsied to Lord Howard. "How do you do m'lord?" "I am great Ms Sinclarie." Lady Hepworth showed the guests inside. Castle Howard was decorated and dripping in elegance and luxury. The guests waited in the Library. The guests were highly distinguished and Elizabeth had an inferiority complex. "What will I do among all these distinguished people brother? I do not even have a goldmine nor a bank balance of a billion pounds." "Yet you have a brother who has both, a billion pounds and..well not exactly a gold mine but I have scored one out of two so yeah you have me and you are here as my sister, is it not enough for you to be here?" "It is but...." "Liz, today is Christmas, no hard feelings, enjoy the party!" Just as Sinderby wanted to walk away to get a glass of a cocktail he met General Greenstone of the '1st The Queen's Dragoon Guards'. Greenstone and Sinderby were together in school and they were best friends. Alastair, Sinderby and Greenstone were called the "Boxer Boys" in school due to their boxer-like appearance. Seeing Greenstone, memories of his early life flowed in Sinderby. He walked up close to him, "Greenstone, do you recognize me?" "I have seen your face somewhere, have I, not sir?" "You certainly have seen my face, old chap, I am Sinderby!" "Sinderby.... Oh, Are you who I think you are?" "Yes Stone, yes!" They both hugged each other and for once in his life Greenstone shed a tear. "How are you dear chap? How the bloody hell are you?" "I am fine and it is General Greenstone now." "I see. I last remembered seeing you as a Private and now you are the General. Time flies quickly." "Yes, dear man and what have you become now?" "Oh, I run a business, nothing much. Have you met Elizabeth?" "You mean 'that' Liz?" "Yes, want to meet her?" "Sure why not." But he had to gulp another glass of whisky before meeting her.

"Sister, surely you must remember Greenstone? Now he is General Greenstone." Elizabeth recognised him immediately and he was the only friend of Sinderby with whom she felt comfortable. She smiled and lent him her hand for a shake. "It has been a long time since we met General, How is your family?" "They are good...um... can I ... well never mind." "No, I insist, do carry on general." "Well.... Can I call you Liz?" She burst into a ripple of laughter and the General was confused about what to do. "Of course, you can! I did not for a minute think you would hesitate to ask me this!" The butler announced that dinner was ready and all the guests went inside the dining room led by Lady Howard. Lord Howard was sitting in the first chair and to his left was Sinderby. On the other side of the table was Lady Howard and to her right was Elizabeth. General Greenstone was bang opposite Sinderby. Lord Howard rose from his seat, "Lords, Ladies and Gentlemen, may I have your attention please?" The room that was filled with chatter and gossip suddenly went silent. "We have gathered here on this auspicious day of Christmas to celebrate the birth of our Lord, Jesus. May we enjoy this gathering here with the fine dinner that has been laid out in front of us and pray to him to protect us from evil and we will all support him to make sure that truth wins! Amen." The guests repeated Amen and waited for Lord Howard to take the lead. He took his cutlery and treated himself to a cured prawn. With the flow of the dinner, Lord Howard asked Sinderby, "Mr Sinderby, I have never heard about this 'sister' of yours. Who is she?" Sinderby laughed and replied, "She is not my biological sister nor are we cousins m'lord well... it is a huge story." Lord Howard suggested, " Why not amuse the guests with it after dinner? It will help us shed some time in the long wait to celebrate Christmas end?"

"Sure m'lord."

He glanced towards Elizabeth only to understand that Lady Howard also had the same doubt. After filling their stomachs the guests came to the grand library of the castle. Impatient to hear the mystery of Sinderby's sister, Lord Howard said, "Distinguished guests, to help us get past this long wait Mr Sinderby has offered to tell us in great detail I suppose about his sister!"

Sinderby stood up and came to the middle of the hall. He glanced at Elizabeth who nodded with a smiling face- the nod that approves the loyal subordinate to reveal the state secrets.

Sinderby started, "I was not born a single child rather I had a sister who was born before me. She was a year older than me and we enjoyed our days together. She was named Sophie after my Irish grandmama and indeed she was as beautiful as the flowers in an Irish garden. We fought with each other and we hugged each other. One day when my family was travelling we met with an accident. I had a fracture and my parents were safe with minor injuries but my sister..." He stopped to make a small pause, took out his kerchief and wiped the one tear from his left eye. It took him a minute to regain his composure. All the guests were glued to his speech and Lord Howard used the pause to have a whisky to help him digest this sorrow. "...She burnt in front of my eyes and I stood there seeing her. I still could not understand why I did not cry or weep when I saw that view. Maybe I was stronger than what I am now? Since I was 4 years old then, my parents moulded me to grow as a single child. I quite forgot her till my 8th grade. I occasionally remembered her during her death day every year but it was not much. When I was in 10th grade, however, I felt that my parents were too old to understand my way of life. I wanted a person who was older than me but had faced the things that I may face in a relatively short period. I had a cousin but she was a decade older than me and we mostly spoke through letters. One fine day my teacher gave my name for a MUN competition and I saw my participants, that was when I saw Elizabeth, at least her name. We were to be double delegating representing Finland. We met with each other and practised, took notes and prepared questions. We won that MUN and we partied all day. After that, I got her mail id and we chatted day and night. We became good friends. When spent an hour after school playing in the park nearby and cycled back to our houses chatting. She was a good friend of mine. For her birthday she had called me to her house. She introduced me to her parents and we- her parents especially her father and me spent hours discussing business. I say for sure that her father liked me. He said to me that he saw me as his son. Immediately I got an idea. I wanted a sister and Liz's dad saw me as his son. The next day in school I hesitated and asked her if she would accept me as her brother? She rejoiced and accepted my proposal. We were still in school but I lifted her high in the air and circled in joy. I always saw her as my sister and respected her and she cared for me like her own brother. She even made me accept her own younger brother as my brother. We loved the time we spent before we made the biggest blunders of our teenage."

Sinderby still remembered what happened then and all the visuals were etched in his memory. He saw what he told to guests and he saw this- He saw Elizabeth always chatting with his best mate Alastair in school. He understood that something was the matter and approached her. "Hey, sis!

You always seem to be speaking with Al, is anything the matter?" She hesitated for a minute and said, "Well you see I feel like he is The One for me. Could you help me in this matter?" Sinderby rejoiced like he never had. "I was waiting when a sibling of mine would ask me this question! Now that you have rested this is my capable hands, sit back and just enjoy the show!" She kissed him on the cheek and they both cycled away. Standing behind a concrete pillar Alastair had a clear view of what Sinderby and Elizabeth were doing and he saw her kiss him. He could not bear it. He loved Elizabeth dearly and to see her kiss another boy just broke his heart. He was not aware of the fact that both of them were in a sister-brother relationship. He could not digest this and he was engulfed in a fit of anger. In anger, he took a decision which brought havoc to this lovely sister-brother duo. The next day Sinderby tried to speak with Alastair but he would not listen to him. He kept moving away from him and occasionally hit Sinderby. Sinderby was confused not knowing what to do. He thought that Alastair was in a bad mood and that he would come back to his senses if he is given a day.

That evening when Sinderby went to leave Elizabeth in her house he saw her father standing out. He could not deduce why was he standing there. He was even more confused to see him with a baseball bat. Sinderby stopped his cycle and asked him, "Good Evening Sir! Going for a game of baseball?" Elizabeth realised something was wrong here. She had never seen her dad play a game of baseball. Before she could spit it out her father raised the bat in the air and gave Sinderby a blow to his chest. That single blow was enough to make him stumble and lose his balance and he fell. Before Sinderby could understand what was going on he was dealt with another blow temporarily incapacitating his limbs. He wailed in such excruciating pain. Elizabeth could not bear this sight and ran to her father, "Daddy what are you doing?" "Leave me alone!" came back the ferocious reply. Sinderby gathered all the energy left in his body and asked him, "Why are you hitting me so mercilessly sir? What have I done?" "What have you not done to me and my daughter you bloody son of a bitch!" Sinderby could not understand and before he could ask the next question another blow landed on his belly making him cough and gasp for water. Elizabeth was in tears to witness all this and she was standing there helplessly. When she came forward to offer him some water her dad pushed her to the side. He finally said to him, "I saw you as my son you bastard! But you kissed my daughter and physically touched her in an uncivilised manner! I thought of you as a true gentleman and is this how gentlemanly you are? Do not be in my sight!" He grabbed Elizabeth by her hand and dragged her inside the house and shut the doors. Elizabeth denied all that physical touching. She said that she kissed him and that too on the cheek and he never behaved in an ungentlemanly manner. Her father however refused to give her statements the slightest consideration.

Sinderby stood up and his knees failed to support his weight. Thankfully he carried a small bottle of whisky, compliments of his father. He gulped it down and it provided him with enough strength to cycle back to his home. His parents were out of town and would return after a week. He called the medics and got his wounds healed. The next day when he went to school Alastair came to meet him. "I think that should serve you enough buddy!" Sinderby could not understand him. "What do you mean Al?" "I refer to yesterday's beatings!" He laughed at Sinderby. "What!" "Yes. I saw her kissing you the day before yesterday. She is my chic and how do you think I would let her kiss you chap? Eh? I went to her father and said that you had been dirty with her and he was foolish enough to trust me." Sinderby was raged but he controlled his anger. "Al, buddy, she and I are siblings. She loves you and I wanted to speak to you on her behalf. She kissed me, yes but it was a sister kissing a brother. What you had done for that, dear fellow is unforgivable!" Alastair was as white as a piece of paper and he knew that he had done a blunder, the biggest blunder of his life. "I am sorry Sinderby, I am sorry! Please forgive me" It was by now too late and Sinderby stepped out of the corridor. Suddenly he saw Elizabeth coming out of her class towards him. He was at first happy but then he decided that speaking with her after yesterday's episode is nothing but a waste. He lowered his head and wanted to walk past her. She stopped him. "Sinderby, are you all right?" He dearly wanted to speak with her but decided against it. He kept walking ahead. She assumed he was angry with her and she was sad for him. Since that day, her father used to come to pick her up and Sinderby thought it best to not even meet her so that her father could be happy with her. That was the last since they spoke. She would always come forward to talk with Sinderby, but he would simply lower his head and move forward. The next year both of them took different groups and they never saw each other. It is only now, after 25 years they are seeing each other.

"And that Lords, Ladies and Gentlemen is the story of how I met my sister." By the time he ended speaking all the guests were in tears. Lord Howard patted Sinderby on his back. Elizabeth stood up and walked towards Sinderby, held his hands and said, "All brothers speak up for their sisters to protect them, but my brother refused to speak with me just so I could be happy. I have a brother who forgave his happiness so that I could be happy." She poured him a glass of champagne and he accepted it. Suddenly he felt the pain, a drastic pain in his chest. For him, this was a blow that he could never manage. He looked as if he had seen all his dead ancestors come back to life to have tea with him. She was his only one and he had spent a great many days with her. This was the last thing he had expected in his life. His past flashed in front of his eyes where he stood in the middle of his school corridor unable to show any emotions. He called Elizabeth and whispered in her ears, "I am happy to have a sister and I am lucky to have you as my sister." These were his final words before he breathed the last. This was the sister's turn to see the brother die. He held her hands tightly even after his heart stopped and the champagne glass was held tightly too- two things he loved the most. She did not weep. She backed away slowly taking one step at a time. Greenstone took over. "Sinderby wanted to be buried in Westminister Abbey. I will do all the necessary steps. Please excuse me Lord Howard, Lady Howard. Lady Howard suggested that Elizabeth spend the night in the Castle. She went to bed, without weeping or shedding a tear. The next morning news of the death of Sinderby was announced and his casket was lowered into the grounds of Westminister Abbey.

Elizabeth made a small speech.

"Ladies and Gentlemen, thank you for gathering here. My brother

Sinderby was a gem of a person. He loved me and when I showed

Him my love he could not bear it and died due to a happy heart

Attack. Let me take this moment to cherish him and love him."

She said all this without crying and the guests observed a moment of silence for Sinderby.

Elizabeth got into Sinderby's car and before she could close the door, Will came running to her. "Miss Elizabeth!" He panted for breath. "What is it, William?" "Sir had a letter for you, ma'am. I was to give it to you when he died." Elizabeth opened the sealed envelope and read the letter.

All it said was, "Dear Elizabeth, I appoint you as the sole owner of my inheritance and the next chairman of Sinderby corporation. Enjoy." She showed it to William. He was surprised, he went without saying a word and came back with a file. He sat in the car's front seat and several other SUVs came in front and behind them. He closed the door and said to her, "Good Morning ma'am. Business as usual. The stock price has slightly gone down and the first thing on your agenda today is to chair the annual board meeting. Be advised item 7 is a bit risky." She nodded and the motorcade drove to the Headquarters of Sinderby Corporation.

9 798886 679588

Printed by Libri Plureos GmbH in Hamburg,
Germany